SECRET of the HAUNTED HOUSE

Written by Fran and Lou Sabin

Illustrated by Irene Trivas

Troll Associates

Library of Congress Cataloging in Publication Data

Sabin, Francene.
   Secret of the haunted house.

   (A Troll easy-to-read mystery)
   Summary: The Maple Street Six club visit a
haunted house and find a mysterious message.
   [1. Mystery and detective stories. 2. Clubs—
Fiction] I. Sabin, Louis. II. Trivas, Irene, ill.
III. Title. IV. Series: Troll easy-to-read mystery.
PZ7.S1172Se   [E]   81-8751
ISBN 0-89375-598-2 (lib. bdg.)   AACR2
ISBN 0-89375-599-0 (pbk.)

10   9   8   7   6   5   4   3   2

SECRET of the HAUNTED HOUSE

Eddie
Sam
Sue
Annie
Sarah
Mike

the Maple Street Six

Everybody said the old Smith house was haunted. That did not frighten Mike.

"There is no such thing as a ghost," he said.

"Then why won't anybody go in there?" Sue asked.

"Because they are scared to," Sam said.

"Well, I'm not," said Mike. "I'll go in any time."

"Okay, I dare you to go in tonight," Eddie said.

"Okay, I will!" Mike answered.

"That's not fair," I said. "The Maple Street Six stick together. If Mike goes, we all go."

I am the president of the Maple Street Six club. My name is Sarah. I asked for a vote. We all voted to go into the Smith house.

"We need flashlights," Annie said.

"And food. Don't forget food," Sam said.

"For hungry ghosts?" Sue asked.

"No, for me," Sam told her.

After dinner we met at the clubhouse.
Eddie, Annie, Sue, and I had flashlights.
Sam had a big sack. In it there were
apples, cookies, a bag of pretzels, and two
salami sandwiches.

"Oh, look. Sam brought food for all of
us," Sue said.

Sam's face turned red. "Well, uh . . .
You see . . . I mean . . ."

"Never mind, Sam," I said. "We won't
want any food—unless we get stuck in the
house all night."

Sam smiled. He hugged the sack to
his chest.

Just then Mike rushed in. He was holding a baseball bat.

"Isn't it a little dark to play baseball?" Annie asked him.

"You told us you weren't scared," Eddie said. "What is the bat for?"

"Well, I couldn't find a flashlight," Mike said. "Anyway, I know that Sue is scared. So I took the bat to protect her."

"Sure," said Eddie.

"I think that was very nice of you, Mike," Sue said.

"All right, Maple Streeters," I said. "Let's go."

Nobody had lived in the Smith house for years. The big garden was filled with junk. There were tin cans, a wagon with no wheels, an old kitchen sink, car tires, and a rubber boot. The weeds were taller than any of us.

The house was just as bad. The front steps were broken. The windows had holes. The whole place looked sad.

Right in back of the house there were woods. We did not want to go back there.

"Come on," said Annie. "The front door is open."

She turned on her flashlight. We followed her along the weedy path, up the broken steps, to the open door. *Scritch-scritch.* It came from behind the door. *Scritch-scritch.*

"What was that?" Sam gasped.

"There *is* a ghost!" Mike cried.

"I'm getting out of here," Sue whispered.

Suddenly, a flash of fur flew through the door. It was a cat.

"There's your ghost," I said.

I led the way inside. It was dark and
gloomy. We shined the flashlights all
around. Cobwebs hung everywhere.

"*Achoo!*" The dust made Sue sneeze.
And that made Eddie jump.

"There's no furniture or anything," Sam said.

"Yeah, there's nothing here," I said. "Let's go home."

Annie shook her head. "Wait a minute. What about upstairs?"

"Let's have a pretzel first," Sam said. "I have plenty for everybody."

Sam dug into his sack. He gave each of us a pretzel.

We took a long time to finish the
pretzels.

"Okay, gang. Upstairs," Mike ordered.
He pointed at the stairs with his baseball
bat.

We stayed close together. The steps
creaked under our shoes. The flashlights
made big, scary shadows on the walls. I
did not like it one bit.

We went into a room. It was empty.
So was the next room, and the one after
that.

"See, there are no ghosts here," Mike
said. "We proved it."

"Not yet," Annie said. She shined her
flashlight at another door.

We walked behind Annie into the last
room.

"I guess a boy used to sleep here,"
said Sue.

"All right, great detective," said Sam.
"How can you tell that?"

Sue showed us the wallpaper. It had pictures of wooden soldiers marching.

"Aha! You used your head, Sue. That is an important clue," Eddie said, using a deep Sherlock Holmes voice. "Now I will find a clue, too," he said.

Eddie grinned at us. Then he stamped around the room. He stared at the ceiling and said, "Ahhhhhhh." He stared at the floor and said, "Hmmmmmmmmmm."

Then he took a really heavy step. A floorboard flew up. Smack! It hit him right in the nose.

"*Ooooohhh!*" Eddie groaned.

"That's using *your* head," Sue said.

"Are you all right?" Mike asked.

Eddie nodded. He rubbed his nose.

Suddenly, Annie jumped up and down. "You did it, Eddie! You *did* find a clue!"

Annie shined her flashlight at the broken floorboard. We all crowded around and looked. We saw a piece of paper in the hole in the floor.

I picked up the paper. There was writing on it. The paper was very old. The writing was hard to read.

"I have an idea," Annie said. She held the paper over her flashlight. That made the writing easy to read.

"What does it say?" asked Sam.

Annie read the note out loud. "DEAR FINDER: WE ARE MOVING FAR AWAY. I PUT ALL THE TREASURE UNDER THE OAK TREE IN BACK. JOHN SMITH."

"Treasure. There's buried treasure in back of this house!" Mike whispered.

"Wow! We're going to be rich!" Eddie shouted.

"Yahoo!" yelled Sue.

"Let's get out there and start digging," I said.

Sam held up a hand. "Not so fast," he said. "Where are you going to dig? There must be a hundred oak trees in back of the house."

Sam was right. We all agreed the best thing to do was talk it over—back at the clubhouse.

We sat around the clubhouse, thinking.

At last, Sue said, "I bet it's a trunk full of money."

"Or a box of jewels," said Eddie.

"I think it is silver and gold," said Annie.

"I think it is time to eat," Sam said.

Sam opened his sack of food. "Here, everybody. Have some."

We ate and talked about the treasure.

Mike wanted to build a new clubhouse with it.

Annie wanted to buy a big sailboat.

"We could use the money to go to the North Pole. With sleds and dogs," said Sue.

"First, we have to find the treasure," said Sam.

"Let's meet in front of the Smith house tomorrow morning," I said. "Ten o'clock. Bring shovels and lunch."

Everybody got there early. We walked around to the back of the house. The sun was shining. Even so, the place looked spooky.

"Now, let's find an oak tree and start," said Eddie.

"Here's one," Annie called out.

All six of us dug up the ground around Annie's oak tree. No treasure.

We dug near another oak tree—and another—and another. We dug a lot of holes. But we did not find anything.

"Gosh, this is hard work," Mike panted.

"It must be time to stop and rest," said Sue.

"And eat," said Sam.

And that is just what we did.

After lunch, I was looking for more oak trees. Then I saw *them!* Holes. Lots of holes in the ground. Somebody else was digging for the treasure!

"Maple Streeters, come here!" I called as loud as I could.

They all rushed up. Everybody saw the holes.

"I bet the treasure was found already," Mike groaned.

"We're too late," grumbled Sue.

"A million dollars . . . gone," wailed Eddie.

We felt glum. "Let's go home," Annie said.

"You said it," Sam answered. His face brightened. "Hey, we didn't have any dessert. You can all come to my house for ice cream."

Suddenly, we heard a sound—like somebody walking in the woods.

"Quick, everybody hide," Sue said.

We ducked behind some bushes and held our breath.

Then we saw him—a big man carrying a bucket and a shovel. He had a long face and a shaggy head of hair.

I giggled. I could not stop myself. Then Mike giggled, too.

"Who's that?" the man said.

We stopped giggling and did not move.

"I said, who's that?" the man asked again.

"*Whoooooooo*. It's the ghost of the Smith house. Beware!"

That was Eddie, the club comic. I did not think he was being very funny.

The man came closer. He peered into the bushes. "Come out," he said. "I won't hurt you."

Eddie stood up. He was shaking. "I didn't mean any harm. Honest, mister," he said.

"What are you doing here?" the man asked.

"We found the note," Eddie told him. "So we came out here to dig. We're looking for the same thing you are."

"We?" the man said. "Are there other people with you?"

I stood up. "Yes, there are six of us," I said, trying to sound brave.

The other kids came out of hiding. "And our parents know where we are," Annie said.

"So don't try anything," Mike added.

"Try what? Looking for what?" The
man looked puzzled. Then he laughed, and
said, "Oh, I see. You are playing games
with me."

He started to walk away.

"Just a second, mister. What are you
hiding in your bucket?" Sam asked.

"Yes, let us see what the treasure
looks like," Sue said.

She walked over to the man and looked into the bucket.

"Yecccch!" she said, turning away.

We hurried over to see what the man had.

"Worms!" shouted Annie.

"Worms! What kind of treasure is that?" Mike asked.

"I wouldn't call them a treasure," the man said. "But they are great for fishing." Then he asked, "What treasure are you looking for?"

We told him about the note in the Smith house, and the oak tree, and the holes we dug.

The man smiled. Then he started to chuckle.

"Come with me," he said. He waved at us to follow him. "I think I can solve your mystery."

We walked a short way into the woods. Then the man stopped. He was under a really tall oak tree. Next to it were three large rocks.

"Okay, kids," the man said. "This is it."

He began to dig a deep hole between the tree and the rocks. Soon we heard *clink*. The man put down his shovel. He put both hands into the hole and took out a rusty metal box.

The man put the box on the ground. "Here is the treasure," he said.

He opened the box. Inside were flat pieces of stone. They rattled when he shook the box.

"That doesn't look like treasure to me," said Sue.

"These are real Indian arrowheads," he said. "They were worth a lot to the boy who buried them."

Eddie's face had a strange look. "And your name is Smith," he cried. "Right?"

The man grinned and nodded.

"Boy, you really are a detective," Annie said to Eddie.

"Yes," I said. "How did you know his name?"

"It wasn't hard," Eddie told us. "The person who wrote the note hid it in the floor. And nobody saw it until we found it. But this man knew where the treasure was buried. So he has to be the one who wrote the note."

"He is John Smith," said Sam. "All grown up."

The Maple Street Six had made Mr. Smith very glad. "For many years I forgot that note," he told us. "I wrote it a long, long time ago, just before my family sold the house and moved across town."

I picked up some of the arrowheads. I liked the way they looked and felt.

"Are they worth a lot of money?" I asked Mr. Smith.

"No. But they are nice to have," he said. "Why don't you kids keep them?"

"Gee, thanks," Sue said. "They'll look neat in the clubhouse."

Then Mr. Smith said he would like to give us a reward for helping him to remember his buried treasure.

"What would you like?" he asked.

"A chocolate ice-cream soda," said Sam.

We all agreed.

"Then sodas it will be," Mr. Smith said. "Come with me."

And we did.